From the Brothers Grimm

*A Contemporary Retelling
of American Folktales and Classic Stories*

From the Brothers Grimm

A Contemporary Retelling
of American Folktales and Classic Stories

Tom Davenport and Gary Carden

Fort Atkinson, Wisconsin

Published by Highsmith Press
W5527 Highway 106
P.O. Box 800
Fort Atkinson, Wisconsin 53538-0800

The paper used in this publication meets the minimum requirements of American National Standard for Information Science - Permanence of Paper for Printed Library Material. ANSI/NISO Z39.48-1984

Library of Congress Cataloging-in-Publication Data:
Davenport, Tom.
  From the Brothers Grimm: contemporary retelling of American
folktales and classic stories / by Tom Davenport and Gary Carden.
    p.   cm.
  Summary: Retells ten fairy tales from the Brothers Grimm, placing
them in the Appalachian Mountains and other American settings
through the text and photographs from the Tom Davenport film versions.
  ISBN: 0-917846-20-6 (alk. paper) : $12.95
  1. Fairy tales--Germany.   [1. Fairy tales. 2. Folklore--Germany.]
I. Carden, Gary. II. Grimm, Jacob, 1785-1863. III. Grimm, Wilhelm,
1786-1859. IV. Title.
PZ8.D194Fr   1992
398.21 ' 0943--dc20   92-30828
                                                        CIP
                                                         AC

Table of Contents

Foreword

About two hundred years ago the Brothers Grimm began collecting oral and literary tales and eventually published them in two volumes as *Children and Household Tales* in 1812 and 1815. The major purpose of their work was to provide the German people with a sense of their customs, beliefs, and history through a wide variety of fascinating tales. The Grimms kept revising these tales in seven different editions to make them relevant to the experiences of the German people, especially young readers, during the nineteenth century. To their credit, their artistic efforts were such that their tales transcended German culture to touch the hearts and minds of readers throughout the world. In fact, there is scarcely a child, storyteller, or folklorist in the twentieth century, who has not been influenced by the Grimms' tales in some way or another.

Yet, many writers and storytellers have endeavored to go beyond the Grimms, not so much because the tales have lost their appeal, but to modify, deepen, and sharpen this appeal for children of today. Such serious and stimulating revision has clearly been the purpose of Tom Davenport's work which has led to a significant "Americanization" of the Grimms' tales, enabling them to take root in our culture and to speak to the concerns and needs of American children.

Working very much in the tradition of the Brothers Grimm themselves, Davenport has collaborated with actors, technicians, storytellers, and writers to explore and bring out essential psychological and social features of the Grimms' tales in his film and printed versions that are directly related to American folklore. He has not "modernized" the tales in a slick, sensationalist manner. Rather he has historicized the tales carefully by giving them American settings from the seventeenth century to the 1940s. By introducing an American perspective, he has shown how such qualities as patience, cunning, and courage have helped his major protagonists overcome poverty, prejudice, and hardship during wars, famine, and depression. Indeed, the agrarian Appalachian background chosen for many of his tales lends them a special flavor that is different from and yet reminiscent of the difficult conditions faced by the German peasants during the Napoleonic Wars and throughout the nineteenth century.

Davenport is interested in how people survive oppression, particularly, how they survive with pride and a sense of their own dignity. Through film and print he conveys these "stories of survival" to give young people a sense of hope, especially at a time in American history when violence, poverty, and degradation appear to minimize their hope for a better future. His story of "Ashpet," based on "Cinderella," is a good example of how Davenport Americanizes a Grimms' fairy tale by retaining the universal struggle to prove one's self-worth, at the same time reshaping and re-invigorating the tale to respond to a contemporary context. *Ashpet* is about a young white woman's reclaiming her proper heritage through the help of a wise black woman, whose sense of history and knowledge of oppression empowers the "enslaved" Lily to pursue her dreams. The action takes place during World War II, when people were making sacrifices and separating, but Lily manages to find the strength to overcome isolation and exploitation by piecing together a sense of her own story. Consequently, Davenport's Cinderella story is no longer history in a traditional male sense, that is, no longer the Grimms' story, or a simple rags-to-riches story. Nor is it a didactic feminist interpretation of Cinderella. Instead, Davenport has turned it now into an American tale about conflicts within a matrilineal heritage in the South, and he shows how storytelling can lead a young woman to recover a sense of her history and give her the strength to assert herself, as many women are doing today. Such self-assertion on the part of women can also be found in Davenport's re-interpretation of "Goose Girl," "Rapunzel," and "The Frog King."

All of Davenport's protagonists want to prove themselves special by overcoming different kinds of adversity simultaneously marked by American history and our present-day struggles. For instance, the soldier figures in *Bearskin* and *Soldier Jack* hark back to the Civil War and World War II, but their use of magical gifts to re-integrate themselves into American society also points to the way many contemporary veterans have been obliged to adjust to American society after the Vietnam War and the Persian Gulf War. The thief in *Jack and the Dentist's Daughter* redeems himself by exposing and undermining class prejudice. The tale of *Hansel and Gretel* raises the issue of poverty during the Depression, but it is also about child abandonment and abuse in our present-day America.

What makes Davenport's films and tales so compelling is that they contain many different socio-historical levels to them and, therefore, challenge young readers and viewers to review American history in light of their current situation. There is a stark simplicity to the images and language of Davenport's stories that recalls the direct manner of the traditional storytellers who have always remained in close touch with the common people. Davenport may use a camera and modern technology to retell the Grimms' tales with an American perspective, but he has not lost contact with the American folk as many filmmakers have done. Rather, his vision of survival and courage in America revives the spirit of the Brothers Grimm as part of our daily struggles. Indeed, his tales and films not only celebrate the creative art of revision that bridges two cultures but also contributes to a unique understanding of American society and history.

Jack Zipes
University of Minnesota

Introduction

When I was a child, my mother would sit on a couch in our living room with my baby sister and me and read fairy tales. Those memories were reactivated in the early 1970s when I bought a reprint of *The Blue Fairy Book* by the Victorian collector Andrew Lang and began reading to my own children. One day my four-year-old son Robert got sick and spent a night in the hospital feeling alone and abandoned in an oxygen tent recovering from croup. When he returned home, I read Robert and his younger brother Matthew "Hansel and Gretel," a story about children who are abandoned by their parents and survived to live "happily ever after."

During this time, I was finishing a documentary film on the Shakers where dialogue and narration were the most important elements. I was tired of talking heads, and I wanted to do a film that told its story in pictures. Days and months passed, and Robert and Matthew wanted to hear "Hansel and Gretel" over and over again. One evening as I snuggled in bed with the boys half reading, half telling the story, it suddenly occurred to me that I could make "Hansel and Gretel" near home on the eastern slope of the Blue Ridge Mountains of Virginia. Here was a story that could be told in pictures!

I imagined "Hansel and Gretel" in images of the 1930s—the Farm Security Administration photos and the pictures in books like *Let Us Now Praise Famous Men* by Walker Evans and James Agee. Born in 1939, I grew up with stories about the Great Depression. My mother's and father's political and social consciousness matured during the 1930s and they had a collection of 78 rpm recordings of folk singers like Woody Guthrie and Leadbelly which I listened to over and over. I was also influenced by the stark, post-war Italian features like *Shoe Shine Boy* and *The Bicycle Thief* that came to theaters in Washington, DC, where my father worked for the Department of Agriculture during the 1940s. I realized that I could make a realistic film literally in my own backyard. The cabins and farms of my rural Virginia community could be "once upon a time" to most modern children who were generations removed from country life.

Like many folktales, "Hansel and Gretel" also spoke to my interests in the psychology of the spirit. I had begun practicing Zen meditation when I was a teacher and Chinese language student in the Far East during the 1960s. In the early 1970s I was reading the works of the psychologist Carl Jung and the mythologist Joseph

Campbell. Jung illustrated his ideas about the collective unconscious with folktales, and Campbell called folktales "the primer of the picture language of the soul."

My wife and co-producer Mimi Davenport and I made *Hansel and Gretel, An Appalachian Version* for under $10,000. I shot and edited it; Mimi did costumes, set design, and sound. Our film followed the story as it appeared in my Pantheon Edition of *Grimm's Fairy Tales* except for my leaving out some of the magical elements in the tale such as the duck that ferries the children across the river to their home territory. We did most of the editing without sound as if it were a silent picture, and the dialogue for the whole movie fits on less than a page.

When we released *Hansel and Gretel, An Appalachian Version* in 1975, it created immediate controversy. The realism of the live-action style and the fidelity to the old folktale upset some reviewers who considered the frightening aspects of film inappropriate for children. However, many other children's film specialists recognized the film's overwhelming popularity with young children, and saw it as a positive breakthrough in children's films.

Emboldened by the success of *Hansel and Gretel*, Mimi and I produced *Rapunzel, Rapunzel* (1979) and *The Frog King* (1980). We continued the realistic, live-action style that I felt most comfortable with. In *The Frog King* we decided to use a real frog instead of a puppet or an actor inside some kind of oversized frog costume. I visited an amphibian specialist at the Smithsonian Institution who told me that they cooled their frogs in the refrigerator crisper where the frogs would go into a state of hibernation and become sluggish and easy to handle. I figured I would need ten frogs in different stages of hibernation depending on what we wanted them to do.

Now I had to catch them. My first idea was to post ads in all the local junior high schools offering $2 for each frog. Instead, I decided to ask Leon Sommers, a twelve-year-old boy who lived on a neighboring farm, to catch some for me. A couple days later, a discouraged Leon showed up with a sack containing only two little frogs. Just before I left for a Zen retreat in New York, I gave him a flashlight and told him to try his luck at night.

When I called later from New York, Mimi told me that Leon had showed up with a sack of 20 frogs! She paid him $40, and from then on, our refrigerator had no room for lettuce. Luckily, I hadn't posted ads—we would have spent all our budget on frogs. *The Making of "The Frog King"* (1981) highlights our frog stars and frog "handlers," and is an interesting account of our early filmmaking efforts.

In 1981, Mimi and I wrote a successful proposal to the Corporation for Public Broadcasting, and received money to do four more folktale adaptations for release to schools via instructional television. We proposed that our series would appeal to all age groups from kindergarten through senior high and submitted *The Frog King* as our pilot. The CPB panel was skeptical, but when they saw *The Frog King* they realized something that I knew: the audience for folktales is not limited to children. Many of the themes and "tale types" they embody are the core plots of popular Hollywood movies and high literature like Chaucer and Shakespeare.

We called the CPB series "From the Brothers Grimm" and continued to follow faithfully the Grimm tales in our productions of *Bristlelip* (1982), *Bearskin* (1982), and *The Goose Girl* (1983). We adapted stories with kings, queens, and princesses to the democratic American environment translating the royal figures of these European fairy tales into the power symbols of the new world—an industrial baron in *The Frog King* and a rich miller/town mayor in *The Goose Girl*. It was much easier to adapt tales from Grimm like "Bearskin" and "Hansel and Gretel" which did not depend on strong class differences based on birth.

For the last tale in the CPB series, we stretched "From the Brothers Grimm" to include a home-grown variant of a Grimm's tale. Related to Grimm's "The Master Thief," *Jack and the Dentist's Daughter* (1983) is a trickster tale best known as "Jack and the Doctor's Gal" in Richard Chase's popular collection of Appalachian *Jack Tales*. Trickster tale types were also collected among rural blacks outside the Appalachian region, and we decided to make the film with a predominately African American cast. *Jack and the Dentist's Daughter* dramatizes the challenge of being young and black in a society where middle-class Babbittry and Uncle Tom-ism conspire to keep the young African American man "in his place."

The ease with which *Jack and the Dentist's Daughter* adapted to a 1930s rural American setting prompted us to consider other American folktales. Supported by the National Endowment for the Humanities, we released *Soldier Jack* in 1988. The story is set just after World War II and features Jack as a kind of Everyman. Our film draws inspiration from the optimistic and good-natured films of directors like Frank Capra. We also set our next film *Ashpet: An American Cinderella* (1990) in the 1940s, this time in the early days of the war when small communities held "victory" dances for soldiers going overseas. Originally I wanted to set the story in World War I, but my costumer said that World War I costumes were hard to find and expensive, so World War II it was. Screenwriter Roger Manley wrote the part of the fairy godmother for the African American storyteller Louise Anderson, who added her own lines to the screenplay and gave the part of "Dark Sally" character development that our previous films lacked.

Finding a lead actress was the major challenge for our tenth "From the Brothers Grimm" adaptation, *Mutzmag: An Appalachian Folktale* (1992). Set deep in the Appalachian Mountains, it required regional accents. After days of disappointing casting calls in Washington, DC, I decided to go to rural western North Carolina and look for Mutzmag and her sisters there. At an open casting call in Asheville, North Carolina, Mimi and I found Robbie Sams, a ninth grader in Madison County High School in the mountains near the North Carolina - Tennessee border. She came with her teacher Sheila Barnhill, who is one of the last authentic Appalachian ballad singers in the United States. I was so impressed with both of them that I asked Sheila to arrange a casting call the next day at Madison County High, and we found most of our other actors there.

Reading or hearing a story is one thing and seeing it fully realized on a screen is another. When you read or listen to a story, your imagination is free to picture it according to your own understanding. A film, on the other hand, pictures it for you. Charlotte Ross, an Appalachian storyteller who has told "Mutzmag" for years, never focused on the fact that the Witch and Giant were cannibals so when she saw my film version, she was shocked. "Why, it's like a horror story!"

Many folktales like "Mutzmag" and "Hansel and Gretel" have dark and frightening elements in them. The plots of these tales are similar to modern day horror films, but with important differences. Whereas the modern horror film often ends with the evil thing lurking around for a sequel, folktales celebrate the decisive victory of the protagonist over the forces of evil. The dark side tests the hero or heroine. Without it, there would be no room for courage and heroism. When you hear "once upon a time," rest assured that there will be a "happily ever after."

The idea for this book was born one day during the silence of a Zen retreat when I should have been pondering serious questions of life and death. I suddenly realized that a Grimm reader based on the series would help popularize the films and would encourage reading and introduce these tales to children and parents. On our casting trip to North Carolina for *Mutzmag* I had met Appalachian storyteller and playwright Gary Carden. I asked him to translate the films back into text, and here is the fruit of our collaboration. It is interesting to see how these old stories change as we adapt them into film and then back into text. Like all good storytellers, Gary gives them a life of their own.

Making films is a collaborative art, and it would require several pages to acknowledge everyone in the casts and crews who helped bring these stories to film. I want especially to thank my associate director Sarah Toth, editors Marcia Neidley Lynch, Randall Horte, and Thom Shepherd; production manager Barry Dornfeld; and our distribution manager and advisor B.J. Williams. Without the sensitivity to character and flair for style and design of my wife and co-producer Mimi Davenport, these films could never have been made. Finally I owe a profound debt to my mother, who encouraged my love for fairy tales in the first place.

Tom Davenport
Delaplane, Virginia

Films in the "From the Brothers Grimm" series received support from the Corporation for Public Broadcasting, The Arthur Vining Davis Foundations, the Virginia Commission for the Arts, and the National Endowment for the Humanities.

1

Ashpet

Once there was a young girl named Lily who lived with her stepmother and her two stepsisters, Thelma and Sooey. The stepmother and her daughters were unkind to Lily and made her do all the hard work. Lily never had any nice clothes, but had to be content with the hand-me-downs of her two stepsisters. Since she didn't have a room of her own, Lily slept in the chimney-corner. She always had ashes in her hair and on her face, so her stepsisters laughed and called her "Ashpet." Eventually, that is what everyone else called her, too.

When Ashpet's father and mother had been alive, she had been loved and cared for. Ashpet still remembered her mother's beautiful dresses, and she had an old photograph of her father riding a horse. After her mother died, her father had married a widow with two daughters. Then her father had died too, and her stepmother told her that she must "work for her keep." So Ashpet cooked, washed and ironed for her stepmother and her two stepsisters. When visitors came to the house, Ashpet was told to stay in the kitchen.

Finally, Ashpet decided to run away. An army base had been established in a nearby town and Ashpet heard that there were many jobs there. Surely there was a job for her! Secretly, she began to pack an old, battered suitcase. But, Thelma and Sooey found out.

"Looky Momma," said Sooey, "Ashpet's going to run away!"

"Ashpet, you ought to be thankful for a roof over your head," said the stepmother. "Now, earn your keep. Iron Sooey's dress like I told you." They watched her after that, and Ashpet saw that she would have little opportunity to escape. She put the battered suitcase away.

Then one day Ashpet heard Thelma and Sooey talking about a dance in town, and they were excited about going.

"Euuuu, there will be soldier boys there!" said Sooey.

On the day of the dance, Thelma and Sooey decided that they needed a magic charm to help them get the attention of the soldiers. They knew that Dark Sally, the old washer-woman who lived nearby, made love potions and charms.

"Momma, can we go over to Dark Sally's and get us some of them sachets that she makes out of roots and things?" said Thelma. "You know that ugly girl that lives behind the school house? She wore one last year and she was married in a week!"

"And she's got twins now, Momma!" said Sooey.

Reluctantly, the stepmother gave the girls money to pay Dark Sally for the charms, and they set off through the woods to her house. Arriving in Dark Sally's yard, the stepsisters called to her.

When the old woman appeared, Sooey said, "We came to get some of your love sachets. Give us two, please."

"What you mean, 'give you?'" said Dark Sally. You want a love potion from me, cross my palm with silver and answer me three riddles."

The stepsisters gave Sally a dime each.

"All right now, tell me what this is," said Sally. *"A white fence with no gate, and when it's closed, it's dark as night. A pink pig with no mate; it opens wide when filled with fright."*

Thelma and Sooey were bewildered. "We don't know," they said.

"Your teeth is the white fence and the pink pig's your tongue," said Sally. "The answer is your own mouth! You're not very good at riddles, I guess. Now listen girls. You don't get a charm until you answer a riddle. What's this? *Two hookers, two lookers, four standabouts and one switchabout.* What is it?"

"We don't know," said Thelma and Sooey.

"It's a cow!" said Sally. "Well, one more chance. *Six men riding six horses through the apple orchard. Each man picked an apple.* How many apples did they get?"

"Six, of course!" said Thelma.

"Sally shook her head. "Just one apple. One man was named 'Each Man.'" Sally shook her head sadly. "You are so pitiful, I'll give you one more chance. *Goes all through the field, goes all down through the woods, goes right up to your steps, but won't go in.* What is it?"

"Each Man?" said Sooey, uncertainly.

"It's your pathway home," said Sally. "You answered no riddles, so you get no love potions. Now, go on home before I turn you into bullfrogs."

Discouraged and angry, the two girls returned home and told their mother, "Momma, Sally won't give us any love potions. She don't like us, but she likes Ashpet. Send Ashpet for the love potions."

Thelma and Sooey told Ashpet that if she brought them the love potions, she could go with them to the dance.

So Ashpet ran through the woods to Dark Sally's house. When Sally saw her coming, she met the girl in the yard and said, "What is this? *Goes all over the pasture, all over the hill, comes way down the road, comes all the way up to the lot, and then, the next morning, it comes and gets up on your table?* What is it?"

"It's milk from a milk cow," said Ashpet. "My mother taught me that one."

"She learned it from me, child," said Sally. "I knew those dumb girls would send you back for their love potions. That's good, because I got something for you. Now, comb my hair while I talk."

"They told me not to be late," said Ashpet.

"The sun will hold still for us," said Sally. "It won't be like any time has passed at all."

While Ashpet combed Sally's hair, Sally talked.

"Are you going to the big dance, child?" said Sally.

"Thelma and Sooey said I could go with them," said Ashpet.

"We'll see," said Sally. "In the mean time, listen now. This love potion is for you. On your way home, you stop at Sweet Water Creek. Pour this potion in the creek, and then you get in and wash from head to toe. When you get out, dry yourself with this towel. Then, hang it on a bush and walk home without looking back."

Ashpet took the potions and did as Sally said, washing the ashes and dirt away in Sweet Water Creek. She arrived home clean and fresh and gave the love potions to Thelma and Sooey.

"Why is your hair wet?" said Sooey.

"I washed it so I'd be ready to go with you to the dance," said Ashpet.

"You didn't think we were serious, did you?" laughed Thelma. "Besides, you have nothing but rags to wear."

"And you have to clean this house and wash the dishes," said the stepmother. "I expect it to be as neat as a pin by the time we get home."

Thelma, Sooey and the stepmother left for the dance. Sadly, Ashpet began washing the dishes. All of a sudden, she looked up and saw Dark Sally standing in the doorway with a lighted lantern.

"Come with me, child," said Sally. "I want to show you something."

She led Ashpet from the kitchen to a secret attic stairway.

"Ain't nobody living today knows about these stairs but me, and now, you."

Brushing aside cobwebs, Sally led Ashpet to an attic room. In the middle of the floor stood a great cedar closet with a heart-shaped lock on it. Removing a key from her pocket, Sally opened the closet, revealing beautiful clothes and jewelry.

"These were your momma's things, child," said Sally. "Now, they belong to you." She reached into the closet and picked up a pair of silver dancing shoes and gave them to Ashpet.

"You must dance and be happy while you're young," said Sally. "Now, you get ready for the dance, and I'll wash the dishes!"

When Ashpet returned to the kitchen, she had on one of her mother's beautiful gowns and the silver dancing shoes.

Sally led her to a big mirror and said, "What is your name, child?"

"Ashpet," said Ashpet.

Sally shook her head. "What is your real name?"

"Lily," said Ashpet.

"Yes," said Sally. "Don't you ever let anybody call you Ashpet again! Now, you go on to the dance."

"How will I get there?" she asked.

Sally led her outside and there was her father's old horse, all brushed and curried.

"You just ride straight through the woods to the other side," said Sally. "You'll come out at the place where they are holding that dance. Now, have a good time, but you have to get home before your stepmomma and stepsisters. Put the gown and shoes back in the cedar closet and put your old ragged clothes back on."

Ashpet, now known as Lily, rode through the woods to the dance. Leaving the horse tied in the woods, Lily entered the dance hall and mingled with the guests.

She saw Thelma and Sooey, but they didn't recognize her. The mayor was making an announcement about all the soldiers that were going to fight overseas, saying this dance tonight was to honor them. He asked a handsome soldier named William to play his saxophone during the next dance. Lily had never heard such beautiful music.

Thelma watched the handsome soldier named William and decided that it was love at first sight. She attempted to flirt with him, but William had seen Lily. From that moment, he seemed to hear or see no one but the girl with the silver dancing shoes. He asked her to dance and Lily accepted. They danced all night. Everyone commented on the beautiful couple. Then, Lily noticed that her stepmother was leaving, and she rushed from the dance hall.

Bewildered, William ran after her. As she climbed on the horse, one of her silver dancing shoes came off. William picked it up and called after her, "I don't even know your name!"

The next day, Lily listened to Thelma and Sooey talk about William and the beautiful girl.

"What kind of clothes did she wear?" said Lily.

"Beautiful!" said Sooey. "No one else had anything like them."

"And was she pretty?" said Lily.

"Yes," said Sooey. "It was the kind of beauty that didn't need make-up or lipstick or love potions."

Lily smiled because they did not suspect that they were now talking to the beautiful girl. A noise from outside caused them to rush to the window in time to see a jeep stop before the house. William got out and came to the door.

"Ashpet, get in the kitchen and stay there. He is coming to see me," said Thelma.

The stepmother opened the door to find William clutching a silver dancing slipper.

"I am looking for the person who lost this shoe," said William.

"That shoe belongs to me," said Thelma.

"You are not the one I am looking for," said William. "Is there anyone else here?"

"My other daughter, Sooey," said the stepmother. William shook his head. "Is there no one else?"

"Only Ashpet in the kitchen," said Sooey.

"Could I see her?" said William.

"No," said Thelma.

William turned away, but then he saw Lily standing in the front yard. She wore an old, tattered dress and carried a suitcase. Rushing to her, William said, "There you are! I was afraid I would have to leave without seeing you. My name is William."

"I am Lily," said Lily.

"Are you the one they called Ashpet?" said William.

"No," said Lily, "Ashpet is gone."

Soldiers called William from the jeep, telling him he must hurry.

"I must go, Lily," he said, "but I will be back." Then, he kissed her. When he was gone, Lily picked up her old suitcase and started walking toward Dark Sally's place.

After the war was over, William did come back. He married Lily, and occasionally, they visit Dark Sally. As for Thelma and Sooey, they are still living with their mother. Without anyone to do the chores for them, they spend a lot of time arguing about whose turn it is to wash the dishes.

2

Bearskin

*In olden times the Devil was recognized
by his green cape and cloven hoof.*

There was once a young man who enlisted as a soldier. He fought bravely during the war and was always in the front when the bullets rained. But when peace was made, he was dismissed. Both of his parents were dead and he had no home, so he went to his brothers and asked them to take him in. "Why should we?" they said. "Your only trade is fighting, and we have no need of that." So, he found himself alone in the world. He had nothing but his gun, so he slung it over his shoulder and started out.

One evening he found himself in the middle of a great field surrounded by trees. Feeling very sad, the young man sat down and thought about his fate. What was he to do without money? He had no trade but war, and now that peace had been made, he wasn't needed anymore. As he looked about him, he suddenly heard a rustling as though the wind had risen, and he sensed that he was not alone. Looking behind him, he saw a well-dressed stranger sitting in the shade of a great tree. The man wore a black beard and a green cape. Smiling politely, he approached the young man, who noticed that the stranger walked with a slight limp. Then, the young man saw the cloven hoof.

"I know what you are in need of," said the stranger. "Gold and possessions shall be yours." The stranger smiled slyly. "But first I must be sure you are fearless, so I don't bestow my money in vain."

The young man laughed. "A soldier and fear? How can those two things go together? Put me to the test."

"Very well," said the stranger. "Look behind you."

The young man turned to find a great bear towering behind him, its arms outstretched to crush him. Quickly, he raised his rifle and fired. The bear crashed to the ground, dead.

The stranger smiled approvingly. "I see you are not without courage," he said. Drawing a knife from beneath his cape, the stranger knelt and began to skin the bear. "But, there is one other condition which you must fulfill."

"If it doesn't endanger my salvation," said the young man, fully aware of who the stranger really was. "Otherwise, I'll have nothing to do with it."

The stranger scowled. "You will have to look to that yourself," he said, "but for the next seven years you shall neither wash, nor trim your beard, nor cut your nails, nor once say the Lord's Prayer. You will give me your jacket, in exchange for which I will give you a cape and a cloak which you must wear during this time. If you die before seven years pass, then you shall be mine. If you live, you shall be free for the rest of your life—and rich to boot."

"Sir," said the young man, "I have risked death many times. We have a bargain." So saying, he removed his coat and tossed it to the stranger. Immediately, the stranger gave the young man his cape, saying, "Wear this cape. When you put your hand into the inner pocket, there will always be money." The young man reached into the pocket and withdrew gold and silver.

The stranger lifted the bearskin, reeking with blood, and said, "And this shall be your cloak. Sleep in it. In no other bed shall you lie." He placed the bloody hide over the young man's shoulders, and said, "Because of this apparel, you shall be called 'Bearskin.'"

Then, taking the young man's coat, the Devil, (for indeed it was he), gave a mocking laugh and vanished into the woods.

And so, the young man went out into the world and enjoyed himself. He surrounded himself with companions who ate and drank at his expense. Spending his money heedlessly in the inns and taverns of the country, he would shout, "With the compliments of Bearskin!"

The first year passed easily, for although his beard became matted with dirt and grease and his nails resembled claws, he suffered little discomfort. But during the second and third years, his companions vanished. Children were afraid of him and he was often pelted with stones in the village streets. He began to have difficulties finding lodging due to his loathsome appearance and smell. Gradually, his body became infested with vermin, rashes and infected sores.

On a night of Bearskin's fourth year, he found himself forced to pay a reluctant innkeeper for lodging in an abandoned barn, agreeing not to show his face inside the inn. Thinking of the years remaining in his pact, he despaired. Reaching into the pocket of the green cape, he withdrew gold and silver coins. Knowing that his money could not buy him true friendship or cure his suffering and loneliness, he flung the coins from him.

At that very moment, he heard the sound of weeping coming from an adjoining stall. Investigating, Bearskin found an old man, who frightened by the appearance of such a shaggy monster, tried to flee. Bearskin spoke gently to the old man, telling him that he was a wanderer without home or friends. He inquired the cause of the old man's unhappiness. Reassured, the old man told Bearskin that his fortune had vanished because of the recent war and the failure of his crops. His three daughters were reduced to poverty and the innkeeper had threatened to send him to prison

because of his unpaid debts. Sadly, he admitted that he could not even pay the innkeeper for his lodging.

"If that is all that is wrong," said Bearskin, "you can stop worrying. I have plenty of money." Bearskin sent for the innkeeper and paid for the old man's lodging. Finally, he gave the old man a purse of money to pay his debts.

Filled with gratitude, the old man invited Bearskin home with him. "I have three beautiful daughters," he said. "I am sure one of them will give you her hand in marriage." The old man looked at Bearskin's filthy beard and tattered clothes. "You do look a bit strange," he said, "but I am sure one of my daughters can set you to rights." The old man's words made Bearskin's heart soar and so he accepted the invitation.

Two of the old man's daughters were anxious to be married. They spent all of their time talking of suitors. When they saw their father's carriage approaching, the daughters did not know what to make of the great shaggy thing beside him in the carriage.

"Perhaps Father has bought me a fur coat," said the oldest.

"If it is a fur coat, it is for me!" said the second daughter.

Indeed, the old man had brought gifts for his daughters, but he had not brought a fur coat. Quickly, he told his daughters that they were no longer poor due to the kindness of a stranger. He told them of his promise: One of his daughters would offer her hand in marriage.

"Even now, he is waiting outside in the hall," said the old man.

"Oh, Papa! Is he a young man?" said the eldest daughter.

"Oh, yes, he is a young man," the father said.

"Is he tall?" said the second daughter.

"Oh, very tall," said the father.

"Does he have dark hair?" said the eldest daughter.

"Dark hair and lots of it!" said the father.

"Is he handsome?"

"Well, he is very kind and generous."

With that the two older daughters rushed into the hall. The eldest daughter was so horrified by Bearskin's appearance, she fled from the room screaming. "I'd rather marry the Devil than marry him," she said.

The second daughter stood her ground, but stated that she would rather be married to an animal that acted like a man than a man that had become an animal.

"But, he is human!" protested the father. "He told me so himself."

But the two older daughters fled, locking themselves in their rooms. Seeing her father's disappointment, the youngest daughter agreed to marry Bearskin saying, "He must be a good man to have helped us. If you promised him a wife, Father, then your promise must be kept." She took Bearskin's hand and smiled at him.

Tears came to Bearskin's eyes. Removing a gold ring from his finger, he broke it and gave half to the youngest daughter. "Take care of this half," he said. "I shall have to wander for another three years. If I do not come back then, you will be free for I shall be dead. Pray God to keep me alive." He went forth to fulfill his bargain.

The youngest daughter dressed in black as though she were in mourning while she waited for the return of her betrothed. Her older sisters teased her cruelly, warning her that when her bridegroom returned, he might crush her in his paws.

"He probably likes you so much, he will just grab you and eat you alive!" said the second sister.

"You must always do what he wants," said the oldest sister. "You know how bears growl."

"I have heard that bears are good dancers," said the second sister. "We'll get to see him dance at the wedding."

But the youngest daughter kept her peace, waiting.

As Bearskin traveled from village to village, he gave money to the poor, asking that they pray that he live to complete his bargain. His heart was filled with joy when he thought of the youngest daughter.

Finally the day came when the seven years were up. Bearskin returned to the field encircled by trees. He heard a sound as though the wind were rising, and turning saw the Devil seated in the shade of a tree. The Devil came forward, scowling, and said, "Here is your coat. Now give me my green one and we are even."

"Not so fast," said Bearskin. "First, you will make me clean." Sullenly, the Devil complied. He cut Bearskin's hair and nails, and hauling water from a nearby stream, he scrubbed away seven years of dirt. When the Devil was done, Bearskin looked like the young soldier of seven years before, except he was more handsome. Going to the nearest town, Bearskin bought himself a fine linen coat and a carriage with four white horses. He went to see his betrothed.

The old man did not recognize the handsome stranger, and thinking him a fine gentleman, introduced him to his two elder daughters. The daughters doted over him, pouring wine and bringing him cakes and sweets to eat. He watched the youngest daughter who sat apart, her eyes downcast and said not a word. Finally, the young man asked the father if he might have the hand of one of his daughters in marriage. When the old man agreed, the two older daughters rushed from the room to put on their finest clothes, each confident that she was the future bride.

When they were alone, the stranger took out his half ring, dropped it into a glass of wine and handed it to the youngest daughter. When she drank the wine, she found the half ring in the bottom and knew that her betrothed had returned. She took the other half which she had been wearing on a ribbon around her neck and fitted the two pieces together.

"I am your betrothed," said the handsome stranger. "I was Bearskin when you saw me last, but now, by the grace of God, I have regained my human form and have become clean again."

Taking the girl in his arms, he kissed her. Just then, the two sisters returned, and when they realized that the handsome young man was Bearskin, they rushed from the house in a rage. The eldest leaped into a well and drowned, and the other hanged herself from a tree.

Later that day, there was a knock on the door, and when the bridegroom opened it, he found the Devil in his green cape smiling bitterly at him.

"You see, I won," the Devil said. "Now I have two souls in exchange for your one."

3

Bristlelip

Once upon a time, a rich man had a daughter who was beautiful beyond all measure, but she was proud and haughty, and no suitor was good enough for her. As time passed, her father became more and more impatient. One day, he invited all of the eligible men to his house, hoping that his daughter would be pleased with one of them.

Alas! Such was not the case. As the proud daughter was presented to each of her would-be suitors, she laughed and teased about the young men that she found so displeasing.

"Really Father," she said, "not one of these men is good enough for me! That one looks like a chipmunk! Oh, and that one is a mere schoolboy! The fat one looks like a wine barrel! This one looks like a basset hound!"

She turned on the last suitor, who had a moustache, and laughed and said, "And you sir, have a bristly lip!" And with that, she seized her little pet dog and ran up the stairs.

Hurt by the daughter's comment, the last suitor, Bristlelip, turned to her father and said, "If I were you, sir, I would marry that girl off to the next peddler that comes to the door."

Frustrated by his daughter's haughtiness and bad behavior, the father said, "By heaven, I'll do it! The next peddler who comes to the door shall have her!"

And so it was that the next morning a peddler with a dark beard arrived at the door, and the father welcomed him. While the peddler was showing his wares to the daughter, the father rushed off to find the minister. Finding him, he returned to the plantation house and told the minister that he should marry the peddler and his daughter. Fascinated by the peddler's jewelry and trinkets, the daughter did not know that the minister was conducting a marriage ceremony. At the moment when the peddler slipped a ring on the daughter's finger, asking if she would buy it, the minister asked if the bride would accept this man for her lawfully, wedded husband.

"I will!" said the daughter, thinking that she had promised to buy the peddler's ring. Too late, she discovered that she was married to the peddler. Her father told her that now that she was married, she couldn't live at home any longer. She must follow her new husband out into the world.

Despite her tears and pleading, she soon found herself on the road with the peddler. As they passed a great mansion, the daughter asked the peddler who owned such a beautiful house.

"That house belongs to Bristlelip," said the peddler.

"And who does this land belong to?" said the daughter.

"Why, also to the man called Bristlelip," said the peddler, and he went on his way singing. Suddenly, there was a great river before them that flowed away through fertile valleys and orchards.

"Whose river is this?" said the daughter.

"It flows through all the lands of Bristlelip," said the peddler.

"Alas, if only I had married him!" said the daughter.

Then the couple entered a great wood and found themselves before a pitiful little shack.

"Oh, whose miserable little hovel is this?" said the daughter.

"This is my house," said the peddler, "where we shall live together."

"Where are the servants?" said the daughter.

The peddler laughed. "You will have to do everything yourself in this house," he said. "Start the fire and fix my dinner."

Since she had led a pampered life, the rich man's daughter could do nothing. The peddler had to teach her how to cook. He told her that she must work for their livelihood, so he brought her rushes to make baskets, but her fingers were too delicate for the rough wood. He tried to teach her to spin, but her soft hands began to bleed. Finally, he told her to try her luck at selling pots in a village market that was nearby.

For the first time, she succeeded. People were glad to buy her pots because she was beautiful. They paid the price that she asked without question. Some even paid for the pots, but did not take them.

One day, as she hawked her wares in the village market, a drunken soldier rode through her stack of pots, breaking them all. Heartbroken, she returned home and told her husband what had happened.

"Don't worry about it," said the peddler consolingly. "I have found you another job where you can get food for both of us."

"Where?" said the girl.

"At Bristlelip's house," said the peddler. "I know the cook and she will give you a job as a kitchen maid."

The girl was horrified. How could a rich man's daughter sink so low? She told the peddler that such work was beneath her.

"Well, you aren't fit for anything else," he said.

And so, the rich man's daughter came to work as a kitchen maid in the house of Bristlelip. She learned to steal food which she would take home for herself and her husband. One day as she was hiding food in her clothes, she heard the servants talking about a ball Bristlelip was holding for all the rich families in the neighborhood. With the other servants, the rich man's daughter hid and watched the dancing. She recognized some of the people as visitors to her father's house.

Suddenly, the servants were discovered by Bristlelip. He dragged the girl out of her hiding place and said, "You've been peeking!" He laughed and said, "The penalty for peeking is you must dance with me." He led her to the middle of the banquet hall and they began to dance. Suddenly, the food that the daughter had stolen fell from her clothing and everyone stared at it.

"So, my little kitchen wench," said Bristlelip. "I give you a job and you steal food from my pantry."

The poor girl wished that she were a hundred feet under the ground. Everyone laughed, and she stood weeping before Bristlelip. She told him that she was married to a peddler and that there was very little food.

"A common peddler?" said Bristlelip. "Is he a good husband?"

"Yes, he is," said the girl, "but I have been a very poor wife."

"Does this sound familiar to you?" asked Bristlelip and then he shouted, "Beautiful tapestries! Jewels and trinkets! All brought back from my travels to Morocco!"

The astonished girl said, "Why, you sound like my husband, the peddler!"

Bristlelip laughed. "I am the peddler!"

The rich man's daughter stared at Bristlelip. "It is you! But why have you done this?"

"I disguised myself because I love you, my dear," said Bristlelip. "I have done all these things to humble your proud spirit. It was I who suggested to your father that you should be married to the next peddler that came to the door, knowing full well that I would be that man! I was the peddler; I was the drunken soldier that broke your pots. And this wedding dance is for you!"

She changed her clothes into a beautiful wedding dress and they danced together. And they may be dancing yet. I wish that you and I had been there to see it.

4

Jack and the Dentist's Daughter

Once there was a poor, young man named Jack who fell in love with Emily, the dentist's daughter. When Jack asked the dentist for his daughter's hand in marriage, the dentist refused.

"Jack, you are just a farm boy and you'll always be poor," said the dentist. "You'll never amount to anything."

Emily protested, telling her father that she loved Jack. The dentist continued to refuse, but told Jack that if he could raise one thousand dollars, he would be more appealing as a son-in-law.

"You show me that you can raise that money and I'll think about you and Emily getting married," said the dentist. "But until then, I don't want to see your face around here."

Hurt by the dentist's words, Jack left, but he resolved to get the money for Emily. Returning home, Jack told his father that he was determined to marry Emily. "I'm going out into the world and find me a job," said Jack. "When I have that money, I'll be back."

"You don't belong with the rich folks, Jack," said his father. "Your place is down here with me."

But Jack was determined to make something of himself. Leaving home, he traveled from town to town looking for work. Days passed and Jack failed to find a job. One night as Jack was walking on a lonely road, it began to rain. Seeing a light in a

lonely farmhouse, he knocked on the door. When an old woman answered, Jack said, "Ma'am, I need a place to stay."

The old woman said, "Well, you don't want to stay here! Don't you know this the home of bootleggers and robbers?"

"I don't care ma'am," said Jack. "I'd just as soon get killed as stay out here and drown in this rain."

The old woman felt sorry for Jack. "If you feel like that, I guess you can come in and rest for a little while." She gave Jack a blanket and let him sleep behind the stove.

Later that night the robbers returned. When they saw Jack asleep, they decided to kill him since he could reveal their hiding place. Jack woke to find himself surrounded by men with guns and knives.

"Please don't kill me," said Jack. "Why don't you let me work for you?"

The robbers considered Jack's offer. "Can you steal?" said one of the robbers.

"I can try," said Jack.

The leader of the robbers' band decided to give Jack a chance.

"Tomorrow there's a farmer taking three cows into market," he said. "I want you to steal one of them, and without letting the farmer know you are doing it. If you can do this, you can be one of us."

The next morning, Jack left the robbers' hideout wondering how he was going to steal the farmer's cow. On the road he found a woman's shoe. After spending several moments looking for a mate for the shoe, he suddenly had an idea. Jack hid in the bushes and waited until he saw the farmer driving his cow toward town. Quickly, Jack dropped the shoe in the road and hid again. Finding the shoe, the farmer looked for the mate, thinking that the pair would make a good present for his wife. When he couldn't find the second shoe, he threw the first away, and drove the cow on down the road. Jack retrieved the shoe and raced through the woods bordering the road, passing the unsuspecting farmer. He placed the shoe in the road a second time and then Jack hid to watch the farmer approach and pick up the shoe. Thinking he had found the mate to the shoe he had found earlier, the farmer tied his cow to a tree and rushed back up the road to retrieve the other shoe. When the farmer was gone, Jack led the cow away.

A few hours later, the farmer started to town to sell another cow. Suddenly, he saw a dead body hanging from a tree limb over the road. Terrified, the farmer rushed back up the road, leaving the cow. Of course, the "dead body" was Jack who had rigged a harness around his body, giving the appearance that he was hanging by his neck. After the farmer ran away, Jack unhooked himself from the harness and led the second cow away.

Later that afternoon, Jack hid in the woods above the road and waited until he saw the farmer approaching with the third cow. Then, Jack began ringing the bells that he had removed from the first two cows. Jack made "mooing" sounds as he moved higher up the mountain. The farmer, thinking that he heard the cows he had previously lost, left the third cow tied to a tree and climbed up the mountain. Jack hid the bells and raced down the mountain. He found the third cow and led her away.

That night when the robbers returned, they found Jack and the three cows outside their hideout. "Why, this boy didn't just steal one cow, he stole three!" said the leader. "Jack, come on in and have a drink! You are a master thief!"

When the leader asked Jack how he did it, Jack replied, "When hunting with a pack of wolves, it is better to be like a fox."

Later that night, while the robbers slept, Jack stole all of their money. Then he drove the cows back to the farmer's pasture. With the robbers' money, Jack went to a nearby town and bought himself a car and some new clothes. He returned home. At first, Jack's father did not recognize the well-dressed man in the new car. But then, Jack said, "What's wrong, Pop? Don't you recognize your own son?" Jack's father laughed at that. Jack told his father about his adventures and how the robbers named him a "master thief."

"Now, all I want you to do is to go up to Dr. Scott's house and tell him that I am ready to marry Emily," said Jack.

Jack's father was reluctant to do what Jack asked. "How am I going to tell them folks that you stole that money?" he said.

"Well, Pop, just tell them the truth," said Jack. "Tell them I have the money and I am ready to set a wedding date."

When Jack's father arrived at Dr. Scott's house, the dentist was working on a patient. When the old man told Dr. Scott that Jack had returned and wanted to marry Emily, the dentist said, "I told that boy of yours not to hang around here because he will never amount to anything."

"Oh, but Dr. Scott, he came back with a brand-new, fancy car and a fine new suit of clothes. Says he has got all the money he needs to marry your daughter," said Jack's father.

"He hasn't been gone long enough to make a thousand dollars," said the dentist. "How did he get the money so quick?"

"Well, he said he stole the money from a bunch of bootleggers and thieves," said Jack's father. "He studied stealing with them and learned a few tricks. He said to tell you that now he is a master thief."

"A master thief, huh!" said the dentist. "Well, you tell that boy of yours that if he wants to court Emily, he is going to have to prove how good he is. Tell him that he is going to have to steal my car out of my barn tonight without anybody knowing it. It isn't going to be easy because I am going to have a couple of mean boys watching out for it. A master thief, huh?" Then, the dentist laughed and returned to work on his patient.

That night the two farm boys that Dr. Scott had hired hid in the barn and waited for Jack. When they heard someone enter the barn, they grabbed the intruder, put a blanket over his head and tied him up. Then, they lit a lantern and discovered that they had tied up an old woman. Of course, it was Jack in disguise. "Unhand me, unhand me," said Jack in a quavering voice. "You have no right to do this to a sickly old woman."

The boys apologized and untied the old woman.

"Fetch me my bag. You have unsettled my nerves something terrible," said Jack. The guards retrieved the old woman's bag which contained a jar of clear liquid.

"What have you got there, ma'am?" said one of the boys.

"Why, just a little bit of ginseng root soaked in some moonshine whiskey. It is good for the nerves." Jack offered to share his medicine with the guards, and in a short time both men were drunk. Jack got into the front seat of the dentist's car, and the guards climbed into the back. They told the old lady about how Jack was supposed to steal the dentist's car.

"Even if Jack came in here tonight," said one of the guards, "he couldn't steal this car."

"Well, why is that?" said Jack in a quavering voice.

"Because we hid the keys, ma'am." said the guard. Then, he pointed to a nearby brick.

"Well, I never would have thought of that," said Jack.

"Ma'am, that's why we put it there," said the guard.

When the guards fell into a drunken sleep, Jack retrieved the key and drove the car out of the barn.

The next morning, Jack got his father to hitch his mules to the car and pull it back to the dentist's house. The dentist discovered that the drunken guards were still asleep in the back seat of his car. The news of how Jack stole the car spread through the town and the dentist was greatly embarrassed.

"Daddy, Jack can come courting now, can't he?" said Emily.

"No," said the dentist, "I never agreed to that."

"Yes, you did," said Emily. "Everybody heard about it."

To add to the dentist's discomfort, the local preacher arrived. When Dr. Scott continued to insist that he would not accept Jack as a son-in-law even though Jack had succeeded in stealing the car, the preacher enjoyed a hearty laugh at the dentist's expense. Dr. Scott became so irritated, he decided to get even with the preacher.

"Well, there is still one more thing that Jack has to steal before I will agree to the marriage," said the dentist. Pointing at the departing preacher, the dentist said to Jack's father, "Let's see Jack steal him! And I expect him to make that preacher look every bit as foolish as he has made me look today."

Late that night, Jack made a pair of angel wings and sneaked into the preacher's backyard. Jack knew that the preacher was

unhappily married, and that he came out each night and drank whiskey from a bottle that he kept hidden at the base of a tree. Jack climbed the tree and waited. Eventually, the preacher arrived, retrieved his bottle and drank. Then, Jack spoke to him.

"Brother Thomas," said Jack, speaking in a high sweet voice.

"Who are you?" said the frightened preacher, staring up into the tree.

"I am an angel sent from God," said Jack. "Don't be afraid Brother Thomas, for the Lord has looked down from heaven to choose a man from among the sons of men! The Lord has chosen you, Brother Thomas, from among all the people of the Earth!"

The preacher's heart swelled with pride. "What does the Lord want me to do?" he said.

Speaking in his angelic voice, Jack said, "Brother Thomas, your days of toil on Earth are over. As in the days of Elijah when the fiery chariots swooped down and carried him to salvation, so too the Lord has seen fit to take you away from the evils of this Earth and to carry you to heaven! And get this! Without tasting death!"

The preacher was beside himself with joy. "I'm going to heaven! Praise God!" Then, he thought for a moment and said, "Are you sure you have the right man?"

"You are Brother Thomas, aren't you?" said Jack.

The preacher was delighted. "Send down those chariots! I'm ready to go!"

"Wait a minute, Brother Thomas," said Jack. "You aren't going to heaven by chariot. Your mortal eyes cannot bear to see the secrets of so great a journey. I will mercifully bring you to heaven in a sack." Then Jack instructed the preacher to go back inside his house and pack his belongings for his heavenly trip.

Shortly afterwards, the preacher returned to the tree with his suitcase and toothbrush. From the top of the tree, Jack pointed to a sack on the ground. "See that sack over yonder? Just ease down into it and we will take off."

When the preacher had climbed into the sack, Jack tied it shut with a rope and began to drag it across the rocky soil to the chicken coop.

"Why is it so bumpy?" said the preacher.

"Wide is the path that leads to destruction," said Jack, "but the road to heaven is straight and narrow."

Then, Jack dragged the sack through a little creek.

"Why is it so wet?" said the preacher.

"We are crossing the river Jordan to that land of promise," said Jack. Then Jack began to sing,

River Jordan is deep and wide,
Milk and honey on the other side.

Then Jack dragged the sack into the chicken coop and the frightened chickens began to flutter and fly about.

"What is that sound?" said the preacher.

"Well now, Brother Thomas," said Jack, "those are the angels of heaven flappin' their wings."

Leaving the sack in the corner, Jack returned home. The following morning, Jack sent the dentist to the chicken coop. Dr. Scott untied the sack and found the preacher inside singing hymns of joy. When the preacher saw the dentist, he exclaimed, "Why Dr. Scott! You made it to heaven, too!"

The dentist laughed heartily.

"I must admit, Jack, you did a wonderful job on the preacher," said the dentist.

"Just like you asked me," said Jack. "Now, I'm ready to marry Emily."

"Oh, that was just a big joke, Jack. I never intended to let you marry my daughter," said the dentist. "However, here is some money for your trouble."

"I kept my end of the bargain, sir," said Jack. "I expect you to keep yours."

The dentist thought for a moment. "All right Jack," he said. "If you want to marry my daughter that badly, I will give you one more task. If you complete this one, I won't stand in your way."

"All right sir," said Jack, "but this is our last bargain."

"This time, you have to get my wife's wedding ring and the sheet off my bed without us knowing it," said the dentist. "Now, remember, if you come as a thief, I will treat you as a thief."

That night, Jack went to the graveyard and dug up the coffin of a robber who had been killed trying to rob the bank. Jack dressed the corpse in his old clothes. Then, he carried the dead robber to the dentist's house. Leaning a ladder against the window of the dentist's bedroom, Jack hoisted the corpse up the ladder and leaned him against the window. The dentist had locked all the doors and windows, and he and his wife had gone to bed. However, the dentist stayed awake with a pistol in his hand. Then, he saw the outline of a man outside his window.

"I know that is you, Jack," said the dentist. "I'm warning you, I have a gun." The dentist's wife awoke.

"What are you doing?" she said. "Put that gun away before you hurt someone." She tried to grab the gun from her husband. When the gun fired accidently, Jack dropped the corpse, climbed down the ladder and hid. The dentist and his wife were very upset. Thinking that he had killed Jack, the dentist opened the window, climbed down the ladder and dragged the corpse away to hide it. After the dentist had vanished, Jack, dressed in a nightgown like the dentist's, climbed the ladder and entered the dark bedroom.

Pretending to be the dentist, he said, "Oh, my Lord! Jack's dead! We killed him!" Then, he said, "What are we going to do with the body?"

"You've got to get rid of it," said the wife. "You have got to bury the body."

"I'll need something to wrap it in," said Jack.

"Here," said the wife, removing the sheet from the bed, "wrap him in this and hurry."

Then, Jack, still pretending to be the dentist, began to cry.

"I feel bad about the ring," he said. "Jack, the poor boy, died for it."

"Here, take it!" said the wife, removing the ring. "Now, hurry."

Jack climbed down the ladder with the ring and the sheet. In a few moments, the dentist came up the stairs.

"Well, that is done," he said to his wife. "I got him buried."

"So quick?" said the wife in amazement. "You just left with the sheet!"

"Sheet!" said the dentist. "Where is the sheet?"

"Why, you took it," said the wife.

"And the ring?" said the dentist.

"Yes," said the wife, "you took that, too."

The dentist shook his head in admiration. "That rascal, Jack!" he said. "He did it again."

And so, Jack and Emily were married. The dentist was very pleased with his new son-in-law, and frequently told his friends, "I always knew that boy would amount to something."

5

The Frog King,
or Faithful Henry

In olden times, when wishing still helped, there lived a rich man whose daughters were all beautiful, but the youngest was so beautiful that even the sun, which had seen so much, was filled with wonder every time it shone upon her face. Not far from the rich man's house was a dark forest, and under an old oak tree in the forest was a little well. On days when it was hot, the beautiful daughter would stand above the well. She would take a golden ball and throw it into the air and catch it. The ball was her favorite plaything.

One day, it so happened that when she held out her hand to catch the ball, she missed it, and it fell into the well. She looked into the well, trying to see the ball, but the well was too deep. She plunged her hand into the water but found only crayfish. She began to cry as though her heart would break. Louder and louder she cried, until suddenly a voice said, "What's the matter? Why, to hear you wailing, a stone would take pity!"

Startled, the girl looked around to see who had spoken, but saw only a frog, who crawled from the well onto a stone ledge where he sat looking at her.

The girl was startled to meet a talking frog, but she replied, "I lost my golden ball in the well."

"I can get it for you," said the frog, "but what will you give me if I fetch it up?"

The girl tried to think of something to give the frog. "Well, there is my dress, or my pearl earrings, or even my necklace."

"I don't want your dress, your pearls, or your necklace," said the frog. "I just want to be your friend. I want to sit at your table, eat from your plate, drink from your cup and sleep in your bed."

The girl hesitated, but then she said, "Yes, yes! Anything, if you will bring back my golden ball." But she was thinking, "I don't have to keep promises to a silly talking frog!"

The frog jumped into the well and, in a few moments, he swam to the surface with the ball. Returning to his ledge, he dropped the ball which rolled to the young girl's feet. Delighted, she retrieved her plaything and ran towards her father's house.

"Wait! Wait! Please take me back with you," called the frog. But the girl returned home, unmindful of her broken promise.

That night the girl's father gave a dinner for his friends, and there was wine, music and wonderful food. As the young girl sat at the table, there was a knock at the door. She left the dinner and went to the door. At first, she could see no one, but then she saw the frog sitting on the doorstep. She closed the door quickly and returned to the table. She was badly frightened. When her father saw how pale she was, he said, "Why are you frightened? Who was at the door? Was it a giant?"

"No, it wasn't, Father," she said. She was very nervous because everyone was staring at her.

"Well then, who was it?" said her father.

"It was just an ugly old frog," said the daughter. Everyone had stopped eating.

"A frog," said the father. "What did he want?"

The daughter told her father about her promise to the frog and the fact that he had retrieved her golden ball from the well. "But I didn't think he could get out of the water. Now he is outside and wants to come in!"

Just then, the frog said loudly from behind the door, "Open the door for me! Remember your promise, my friend to be. Open the door for me!"

"Well, open the door," said the father.

"But Father," said the girl, "he is just a disgusting frog."

"You made a promise," said the father, "and you must keep it. Let him in."

The daughter opened the door and returned to her seat at the table. The frog hopped into the house and entered the room where the guests were dining. Everyone watched as the frog hopped

across the floor and stopped by the daughter's chair, where he sat waiting patiently for someone to lift him up to the table so that he could eat from the young girl's plate and drink from her cup. The father ordered a servant to place a stack of cushions in the chair next to his youngest daughter. The frog was placed on the top of the stack.

"Move your plate closer so we can eat together," said the frog. Reluctantly, the girl moved the plate and the frog hopped into it. Then he hopped about the table, overturning wine glasses and saucers while the guests looked on. Then the frog said to the daughter, "Now, I'm tired and I want to go to bed. Carry me up to your room."

"I won't," said the girl. "You have ruined the party, gotten my clothes dirty and embarrassed me in front of everyone!"

"You must keep your promise," said the father. "Carry the frog up to your room."

Angered and frustrated, the girl picked the frog out of a soup bowl and carried him up to her bedroom. She placed him on her dresser, put on her nightgown and got into bed.

"I want to be as comfortable as you," said the frog, hopping from the dresser to the floor and then to the foot of the bed. "Lift me up into your bed."

"No!" said the girl.

"Lift me up or I'll tell your father," said the frog.

At the end of her patience, the girl picked up the frog and threw him against the wall. When the frog struck the wall, he turned into a young man who looked at the youngest daughter with kind and beautiful eyes. He told her how a wicked witch had put a charm on him and no one had been able to set him free—no one but the youngest daughter. And so it was by her father's wish that the young man became her true friend and husband.

The next morning when the sun rose, a carriage came to take the couple to the young man's home.

In the back of the carriage sat a servant named Faithful Henry. He had been so unhappy when the young man had been turned into a frog that he had an iron band placed around his heart to keep it from breaking. When the carriage had gone a little way, the young couple heard a cracking and thought that the carriage was breaking apart. But, no, it was only the band springing from the heart of Faithful Henry because his master was free and happy.

6

The Goose Girl

Once upon a time there was a woman whose husband had been dead for many years. She had a daughter who was promised in marriage to the son of a rich man who lived a great way off. The woman packed up vessels of gold and silver—everything proper for her child's dowry, and when the hour of parting came, the woman took a knife and pricked her finger. She let three drops of blood fall on a white handkerchief and gave it to her daughter.

"Take this," she said, "it will preserve thee from harm."

The daughter folded the handkerchief and placed it in the bodice of her dress. When the daughter was ready to depart, the mother had two horses brought from the stable. One was for the maid who was to accompany the bride-to-be to her new home; the other horse was white and named Falada. He was greatly valued by the mother for he could talk. The mother told the maid to take care of the daughter and see that she arrived safely.

But the maid's heart was filled with envy, and as the journey progressed, her jealousy increased. After several hours of travel, the daughter grew thirsty. Stopping near a mountain stream, she said, "Maid, I am thirsty. Take my cup and bring me some water from the stream."

At first, the sullen maid did not respond, but when the daughter asked her a second time, the maid said, "If thou art thirsty, get off thy horse thyself, lie down and drink from the river. I do not choose to be thy maid."

The daughter, being of a meek and gentle nature, did as she was told. When she bent over the stream to drink, the handkerchief with the three drops of blood fell from her bodice and was carried away by the racing water. She did not notice the loss of the handkerchief but the maid did. Now she knew that the bride-to-be was no longer protected by the mother's charm.

When the daughter returned from the stream, the maid said, "Your white horse is suitable for me; the nag will do for thee!"

Then the maid seized the daughter and demanded that she exchange clothes with her, saying, "I will be the bride! Swear by all things holy not to tell a single soul. Swear or I will kill thee!"

The frightened daughter swore. And so it was that the maid became the bride-to-be and the bride-to-be became the maid. When the two women arrived at the prosperous farm owned by the bridegroom's father, the false bride was riding Falada and the true bride was riding the maid's poor nag.

The false bride was treated with great courtesy by the bridegroom and his father. Turning to the true bride, who was dressed in the maid's ragged clothes, they asked who she was. The poor daughter was too frightened to speak for she had sworn an oath. The false bride said, "She is merely a serving girl I picked up along the way. Put her to work, for I have grown tired of her." The bridegroom's father could find nothing for the poor girl to do, so he sent her down to tend the geese with a farm boy named Conrad.

Remembering that Falada could speak, the false bride feared that the horse would reveal her true identity.

"During the journey, my horse vexed me," she told the bridegroom. "Wilt thou have him killed?" The bridegroom found the request strange, but the false bride said, "T'is merely a horse! Promise me a favor and I'll give thee one in return."

And so the bridegroom sent a man to kill the horse. Hearing what had happened to Falada, the true bride was saddened. Using the few coins that she had, she bribed a farm hand to cut off the horse's head and hang it above an archway through which she must pass each day. Each morning as the true bride and Conrad

drove the geese to the meadow, she would halt before the archway and say, *"Alas, Falada, hanging there!"*

Falada's head would reply,
Alas, young bride, how ill you fare!
If this thy mother knew,
Her heart would break in two.

After that the true bride continued to the meadow where she and Conrad tended the geese. Each day, the true bride sat down, undid her hair, combed and braided it. Fascinated by the goose girl's beauty, Conrad would try to steal a lock of her hair. When this happened, the goose girl would sing:

Blow, blow, thou gentle wind, I say,
Blow Conrad's little hat away.
And make him chase it here and there,
Until I've braided all my hair
And bound it up again."

When the goose girl sang, poor Conrad's hat would go flying up into the sky, sailing here and there as he tried desperately to catch it. Each day Conrad chased his hat while the goose girl combed and braided her hair. Finally, the unhappy Conrad went to the bridegroom's father.

"I don't want to tend geese with the goose girl," he said. "She makes the wind come up and blow my hat away. There is something strange about that girl. She talks to the horse's head above the archway."

The father was curious about what Conrad had told him, so he ordered the boy to return to his chores as before. The next day, the father hid and observed the goose girl. He heard her speak to Falada's head.

Alas, Falada, hanging there.

And he heard Falada say,

Alas, young bride, how ill you fare.
If this thy mother knew,
Her would break her heart in two.

Following the goose girl and Conrad to the meadow, the father heard her sing:

Blow, blow, thou gentle wind, I say!
Blow Conrad's little hat away.
And make him chase it here and there,
Until I've braided all my hair
And bound it up again."

The father saw poor Conrad trying in vain to catch his hat.

That evening, the father sent for the goose girl. Taking her hands, he said, "These are not the hands of a serving girl. Where are you from? Who is thy mother? Thou can tell me; thy oath will be safe with me."

But the goose girl could not speak, for she had sworn an oath to tell no other person. Sensing this, the father said, "Go to your room. If thou can'st tell no other person, tell it to the hearth."

Hiding in the room adjoining the goose girl's, the father listened. He heard the goose girl approach the hearth and say, "I am deserted by the whole world, but I am the true bride, and she has taken my place by my bridegroom's side. *If this my mother knew, it would break her heart in two."*

Hearing this, the father took the true bride from her room and gave orders that she was to be dressed for her wedding. He immediately sought out his son and said, "Your true bride awaits upstairs. She was the goose girl. Go!"

The goose girl was dressed in beautiful clothes and when the bridegroom saw her, he rejoiced, for her beauty and her virtue

shone from her face. At the father's request, a great feast was made ready, and the false bride was seated on one side of the bridegroom and the true bride on the other. Since the true bride was veiled, the false bride did not recognize her. Then the father rose and proposed a toast to the bride. Before drinking to her happiness, however, he said he wanted to ask her a riddle.

"Once upon a time a princess and her maid were traveling to a distant country where the princess was to be married," he said. "The maid was much older and was sent along to protect the princess as they journeyed through the wilderness. But on the way, the maid beat the princess and would have killed her, if she had not agreed to change clothes. She forced the princess to swear to tell no person of this. When they arrived at the distant kingdom, the young king thought that the maid was his bride. Now, my question is this: What punishment does this maid deserve?"

The false bride perceived no threat and said, "She deserves no better fate than to be stripped naked, put in a barrel studded with nails and dragged by two white horses until she is dead."

Then, the father said, "You have pronounced your own sentence!" And the false bride was taken away and her punishment carried out. The father toasted the true bride and his son. And so it was that the two of them lived together in peace and happiness for the rest of their lives.

7

Hansel and Gretel

Once upon a time, on the edge of a great forest lived a woodcutter and his family. Times were hard and for days the poor man had not been able to find work or sell what little he had gathered from the forest. Food had always been scarce in their house and as time passed what little food they had was eaten. Only flour enough for a few loaves of bread remained. The woodcutter had two children. The girl was named Gretel, the boy Hansel.

The wife was not the children's real mother and she resented having to share what little food there was with them. She hardened her heart against Hansel and Gretel, finally telling her husband, "Tomorrow we will take the children into the deep forest and leave them." The father protested, for he loved his children dearly. His wife said, "It is them or us." The children overheard their stepmother's plans. That night Hansel slipped from the house and stuffed his pockets with white pebbles.

The next day, before the sun had risen, the stepmother woke the children saying, "We are going deep into the forest for wood today. Come along and earn your keep!" They started out for the forest. When they had gone a little way, Hansel began to lag behind, stopping to drop a white pebble on the ground. When his stepmother became suspicious, he explained that he was waiting for his white kitten which he could see on the porch of their cabin.

"You stupid fool! That's no cat. Its just the sun shining on the porch," said his stepmother. "Come on." And so Hansel managed to leave a trail of white pebbles.

When they were deep in the forest, the stepmother ordered the children to lie down, saying that she and the father were going into the forest to cut wood. "Stay here until we come back," she said. The father gave the children pieces of bread that he carried in his pockets. "Come on, husband," said the stepmother, and the two adults vanished into the woods.

Hansel and Gretel fell into a deep sleep and when they awoke, it was night. When the full moon had risen, Hansel took his sister's hand and, following the pebbles, returned the way that they had come. They walked for hours, reaching the cabin after midnight. When their stepmother saw them she said, "What the devil do you kids mean coming in at this hour? Why, we've been waiting up a long time. We didn't think you were ever coming back." Then she added, "Tomorrow we are going out again, so go on and get up to bed." The children clung to their father, but their stepmother said, "Get away from your father and go on up to bed."

This time, the stepmother locked the door and Hansel could not get out to pick up white pebbles. He would have to think of another plan.

When the stepmother came for the children the next morning, she gave them pieces of bread to eat on their journey. Instead of eating his bread, however, Hansel dropped bread crumbs on the ground. This time they were led deeper into the

woods. Again, the children watched their father and their stepmother walk away and vanish. The day passed and the sun set, but no one came to lead the children home again. That night when the moon had risen, they began to search for the bits of bread, but found none. The thousands of birds that lived in the forest had eaten the crumbs as fast as they had been dropped. They were lost at last.

They walked all night and all of the next day but the forest had no end. Tired and hungry, they fell asleep. When they awoke on the third morning, they were weak from hunger. They set out again, walking deeper into the forest.

Suddenly, they broke through the undergrowth into a clearing. Before them was a strange little house. Approaching it, the children discovered that it was made out of gingerbread. The roof was cake and the windows were sparkling sugar. On a table before the door was a cake. Two slices had been cut and placed on plates as though waiting for the hungry children.

"Let's eat," said Hansel. As the two children began to eat the cake, they heard a curious rhyme:

Nibble, nibble little mouse,
Who's that nibbling at my house?

Suddenly the door of the little house opened and an old woman came out. She wore a black dress and shoes with silver buckles. Her great, hooked nose sniffed the air as she approached. Hansel and Gretel were so frightened they dropped what they were eating and turned to run. But the old woman said, "Why, it is two beautiful little children! Don't be afraid! Come inside. I have food and lots of it!" And coaxing Hansel and Gretel through the door she said, "Just this way. Don't be afraid. Follow me."

Once inside, the old woman had the children sit at a little table and she began to place food before them. They ate their fill of apples, bread and cheese. Tired from their long journey, the children fell asleep in their chairs.

The old woman had only pretended to be kind. In actual fact, she was a wicked witch who waylaid lost children. She had built her house to entice them, and once they fell into her hands, she killed, cooked and ate them. Now as she looked at the sleeping Hansel and Gretel, she muttered to herself, "What tasty morsels they will be!"

Dropping a sack over Hansel's head, she dragged him to a little shed and closed the iron-barred door behind him. She went back and awakened Gretel. "Wake up, you lazy girl," she said. The old witch led Gretel outside and pointed to Hansel locked in the little shed. "See your brother? I put him in there because we are going to fatten him up and I'm going to eat him!" Gretel began to cry. "Oh, stop that crying," said the witch. "We have work to do. You are going to help me fatten him up."

Gretel worked for the witch day after day. The best food was cooked for poor Hansel, but Gretel got nothing but scraps. Every morning, the old witch went to the shed and said, "Hansel, hold out your finger. I want to see if you are getting fat." Now, witches

have weak eyes, but like beasts, they have a keen sense of smell, especially for human flesh. Hansel knew the old witch could not see well, so he held out a chicken bone. The old witch would feel the bone and shake her head, wondering why Hansel was not getting fat.

After four weeks, the witch became impatient. Deciding not to wait any longer, she told Gretel, "I'm tired of this. Your brother is as skinny as the day you got here. Fatter or thinner, tonight I'm going to have him for dinner! Now fetch some water."

Gretel began to cry, and the witch laughed at her. "Stop that blubbering," she said. "It won't do you a bit of good." As she thought about the coming feast, the witch cackled and clapped her hands. "Oh, he is going to taste so good!" she said.

After Gretel had filled the kettle with water and lit the fire, the old witch said, "I'm going to bake some bread. I have already heated the oven and kneaded the dough." Then the witch took Gretel outside to a great oven which was so hot, it was spitting flames.

The witch said sweetly, "Gretel dear, would you do something for me? Would you stick your head in the oven and see if the fire is ready?" Gretel knew it was a trap. The witch intended to cook her in the oven as she boiled Hansel in the pot. Gretel said, "I don't know how to open the door."

"Oh, you stupid girl! You don't know anything," said the witch. "Now, watch me. I'll show you how to do it and then you will do it after me. Now you just open the door." The witch opened the door of the oven. "Now, you look at the coals," and the witch leaned into the oven and Gretel gave her a push. The little girl slammed the door shut and ran away as the witch burned to death, screeching. Then, seizing the key to Hansel's shed, she ran and released her brother. She told him that the old witch was dead, and the brother and sister hugged each other and danced about.

Gretel had seen where the witch had kept her treasure. The children found boxes filled with pearls and precious stones. "These are better than pebbles," laughed Hansel. "Let's take some home."

Once more the children set out, wandering for some hours before they came to a river. When they reached the other shore, they found that they had returned to familiar ground. Now the way home was clear. When they saw their father's house in the distance, they began to run, calling, "Father, Father!" The father

heard them calling and rushed to meet them. The poor man was amazed and beside himself with joy. He told them that he had not passed a happy hour since he had left them in the woods. The stepmother had left, and so Hansel and Gretel returned home. Now that they were rich with the witch's treasure, their troubles seemed to end, and they all lived happily ever after in that little house near the forest.

My story's told, there is no more;
But there's a mouse behind the door.
The first of you that catches her,
Can make a great big cap from her fur.

8

Mutzmag

Once there was a widow who lived in the middle of a cabbage patch in a tumble-down shack with three girls. Two of the girls, Poll and Nance, were her daughters by her first husband; but the youngest, Mutzmag, was the daughter of her second husband. He had died a year or two before and had been buried on the backside of the cabbage patch next to her first husband.

The widow and her daughters were very poor. To make matters worse, Poll and Nance refused to work and spent all of their time primping, sleeping and eating. They thought that working in the cabbage patch or helping with the chores was bad for their complexions. The youngest daughter, Mutzmag, had to do all the work. She hoed cabbage, split wood, carried water and cooked. Everything she owned was handed down by Poll and Nance who wouldn't let her go anywhere with them because they were ashamed of her.

One day, the widow fell sick. When she was carried to her bed, she called the girls to her and told them that she was going to die.

"Now, Poll and Nance, I'm gonna give you'uns the cabbage patch and the little house," she said. "Take good care of it, 'cause thet's all I have for you." Then she looked at Mutzmag and she reached in her apron pocket and pulled out an old case knife with a broken handle.

"Mutzmag, all I got left in the world is this old case knife," she said. "I want you to have it. Keep it in your apron pocket, 'cause you never can tell when you might need a good knife." Then she turned her face to the wall and died. Mutzmag cried, for she had loved her mother. The daughters called the neighbors to help with the funeral. They tied the old woman's feet together, placed pennies on her eyes to keep them shut, put her in her coffin and buried her on the backside of the cabbage patch between her two husbands.

Before long, Poll and Nance ate all the cabbage in the patch and decided that they would go out into the world to "seek their fortune." Mutzmag heard them talking and wanted to go with them, but her two half-sisters said she had to stay and take care of the old shack and the patch. Nance, the older half-sister, said, "Mutzmag, you run over to the neighbors and borrow a cup of meal for a johnny-cake. We'll be leaving in the morning."

Mutzmag borrowed the meal, and the next morning, she made the johnny-cake. She asked again if she could go, too.

"No, you can't," said Poll. "We'd be ashamed to have you with us."

But Mutzmag kept begging, and finally Nance said, "Mutzmag, you can go on one condition. Take this riddle down to the branch, fill it up with water and bring it back to the house. If you can do that, you can go."

Since a riddle has holes in the bottom like a sieve, Poll and Nance figured they were rid of Mutzmag. But when Mutzmag got to the branch, she packed the bottom of the riddle with moss and

filled it up with water. When she returned to the house with the water, Poll and Nance were already gone. Mutzmag found a ball of twine on the floor and put it in her apron pocket with her case-knife.

She remembered that her mother always said, "You can never tell when a ball of string might come in handy." Then she set off after her half-sisters.

When Poll and Nance saw her coming, they were none too pleased.

"There is that dirty thing coming after us," said Poll. "What will we do now?"

"Jest be patient," said Nance. "I got a plan."

"I caught the water in the riddle like you said," Mutzmag said when she caught up with Poll and Nance.

"I don't see no riddle with water in it," said Poll.

"Both of ye, jest hush," said Nance who was looking for some way to get rid of Mutzmag. Then the girls came to an old shop house on the road.

"My suitcase is coming apart," said Nance. "Mutzmag, go in that old shop house and see if you can find something to fix it with. I'd go, but me and Poll is a-skeered of spiders."

When Mutzmag entered the shop house, Poll and Nance slammed the door and latched it. "Nobody will find her for a long time," said Nance to Poll. "We're rid of her."

Mutzmag banged on the door and pleaded with her half-sisters to let her out. After a while, Mutzmag remembered her case-knife. Removing it from her apron pocket, she opened the knife and slid the blade under the latch and raised it. Then, she ran after Poll and Nance.

When Poll and Nance saw her coming, Poll said, "Here comes that dirty thing again! Let's jest kill her."

"Well, I don't know about you, but I'm getting awful tired of carrying this suitcase," said Nance. "Why don't we make her carry this stuff for us?"

"But she's so dirty!" whined Poll.

"We could make her walk behind us and tell folks that she is our servant-girl," said Nance.

When Mutzmag caught up with Poll and Nance, Poll told her, "You can go with us, but you have to walk behind us and carry our suitcases like you are our hired girl."

So Mutzmag walked behind Poll and Nance lugging their belongings. They walked a long time. It was getting late and the three girls were cold and hungry when they came to a house. Poll knocked on the door and when a woman opened it, she said, "We were wondering if we could spend the night. We have a servant girl."

But the woman was frightened and refused to let them in the house. "Go back where you come from," she said. "Go back before the dark falls." Then she slammed the door.

"She must be crazy," said Nance. "Let's go on and find another place before it gets dark."

Before long, the three girls were lost. The sun had set when they entered a dark forest where they saw a little log house at the head of a branch. They could see a fire burning through the cracks of the logs and there was smoke coming out of the chimney. When they approached it, a great, black dog on a chain rushed at them. The three girls were badly frightened. Then the door opened. Outlined against the fire in the fireplace was the ugliest woman they had ever seen.

"Well, what do we have here?" she said.

"We are two fine ladies. We have been traveling all day and we are tired and hungry," said Poll.

"We've got a hired girl who will help you take out the ashes, take in the water, fetch wood and kindling, and clean pots and pans," said Nance.

"You come right in," said the woman. "We never turn anybody away," she added smiling.

Mutzmag followed Poll and Nance into the cabin.

"I have three daughters myself," said the woman. "They are already asleep up in the loft." She began to put food on the table. "I expect you all are hungry. I made this big old pot of beans, almost like I was expecting you."

While the three girls were eating, the woman said, "You all must not be from around here." The stepsisters told her that they were "seeking their fortune." Then they ordered Mutzmag to go out and get kindling for the lady.

"Don't be afraid of that old dog," said the woman.

"He's on a chain, Mutzmag," said Poll. "He can't hurt you."

Outside, Mutzmag stumbled over something on the ground and saw that it was a human skull. There were bones scattered everywhere. Returning to the cabin, Mutzmag stoked up the fire. Then she noticed a line of chalk marks on the fireboard. In a while, the woman said, "Well now, I guess you all is tired. You can go up in the loft and find yourself a place in the hay next to my daughters."

Mutzmag followed Poll and Nance up the ladder to the loft. She could see the three daughters asleep and each wore a dirty lace night-cap. They had ugly little faces and too many teeth, and they growled and purred like cats in their sleep. Poll and Nance fell asleep immediately but Mutzmag stayed awake, listening. She thought about the skull in the backyard. She peered through a crack in the loft floor and saw the woman sitting by the fireplace with a basket of bones, whispering to them.

"I remember you," she said. "And you! Fat little boy. Had to chase you around didn't I?" Then Mutzmag knew that the woman was a witch and the bones in the basket were travelers that she had killed and eaten. Suddenly, the black dog barked and the door of the cabin shook and rattled. The witch opened the door and a giant came in, carrying a dead chicken.

"Ssshh," she whispered. "You don't need that." She took the chicken from him and threw it in the corner. "I've got you three fat pullets in the loft."

She told the giant about the three girls. "You go up there and kill them, Toady," she said. "I'll go get some water and then we will cook them."

"Wait," said the giant, "it's dark in the loft. How will I know which are your daughters?"

"My girls are wearing night-caps," said the witch, and she went outside to get water.

The giant was so tall, he could reach up into the loft without climbing the ladder. Quickly, Mutzmag snatched the night-caps from the heads of the witch's daughters and placed them on Poll and Nance. Then, tying a night-cap on her on head, she lay down just as the giant reached through the loft-hole. He groped in the darkness and his hand touched each of the night caps on Poll, Nance and Mutzmag. Then he touched the bare heads of the witch's daughters. One by one, he broke their necks and pulled them down through the loft-hole. He found a piece of chalk and added three more marks to the tally on the fireboard. Mutzmag watched through the hole in the loft floor as the giant went to the cupboard and ate honey which he quickly hid when he heard the witch returning.

Mutzmag used her case-knife to cut up some blankets which she tied together and made a rope. She lowered the rope out the attic window. Then the witch screamed and Mutzmag knew that she had found her daughters.

"You fool!" she screamed at the giant. "You killed the wrong ones! You killed my pretty daughters!" She attacked the giant with a frying pan.

Mutzmag shook Poll and Nance awake.

"Come on," she whispered. "We gotta get out of here."

The three girls climbed down the rope and ran into the forest. Behind them, they could hear the witch and the giant as they fought. They ran all night and at daybreak, they found themselves in a wooded area near a large country farmhouse with a chimney on either end and blue trim around the windows.

"Must be somebody rich lives here," said Nance.

Once more, Poll and Nance insisted that Mutzmag pretend to be their hired girl. As they approached the porch, they saw a man with a gun watching them from a window.

"Don't shoot!" said Poll. "We have been on the run all night."

"We escaped from a witch and her big man last night," said Mutzmag.

Cautiously, the man and his wife invited the girls inside.

"We are what you would call the king and queen in these parts," said the man. "We have been afraid to go out of the house for a long time because of the witch and the giant."

Poll and Nance told the king and queen about their narrow escape. When they told it, they made it sound like they were the ones who had discovered the witch's plans and switched the nightcaps to their own heads. Poll and Nance pretended that Mutzmag had nothing to do with it.

The king told the girls that the witch and the giant had been killing and eating travelers for a long time. They offered the girls one thousand dollars if they could kill either the giant or the

witch. When Poll and Nance pretended to consider the king's offer, he added, "That giant stole my white horse, Ten-Mile Stepper. I would give a bushel of gold to get him back."

That night each of the three girls had their own bedroom. Mutzmag lay awake thinking about how wonderful it would be to have her own bedroom. She thought about the fine house owned by the king and queen. She tried to think of a plan to get rid of the witch and the giant, and how she might get Ten-Mile Stepper and return him to the king. Finally, she fell asleep.

The next morning, Poll and Nance were gone. They had slipped out in the night. Mutzmag stayed on and worked for the king and queen.

"I've got a plan to get rid of the giant and the witch, and get your white horse back," she told the king one night.

"I'll give you a thousand dollars each for either one of their heads," said the king, "and I'll give you an extra thousand dollars if you bring that horse back."

"I'll need a sack of salt," said Mutzmag.

Mutzmag left the next morning. Carrying a sack of salt, she walked all day and got to the witch's house just after dark. She hid behind the cabin away from the great black dog. She climbed the roof and hid behind the chimney.

When the giant came home that night, the witch was cooking squirrels. When she hung the kettle in the fireplace, Mutzmag poured salt from her sack down the chimney into the kettle. The giant and the witch were arguing and did not notice the salt pouring down the chimney. When the giant tried to eat his squirrel stew, he spit it out.

"Phaaa! What are you trying to do, poison me?" he said. "It's too salty."

"Too salty!" said the witch. "Why I just put in a pinch."

"Get me some water!" shouted the giant.

So, the witch took a lantern and a bucket and left the cabin to get water from the spring. Mutzmag climbed down from the roof and ran into the woods where she stretched string between two saplings at the edge of a cliff.

"Like Maw told me," thought Mutzmag, "you never can tell when you might need a ball of string."

When the witch approached, Mutzmag threw a rock and shattered the witch's lantern. Peering into the darkness, the witch recognized Mutzmag.

"Well, if it ain't the little hired girl," she said. "You killed my daughters and now I'm gonna kill you."

Mutzmag ran from the witch, luring her toward the cliff. The witch rushed at Mutzmag, tripped over the string and fell to her death. Knowing that the king would want proof of the witch's death, Mutzmag took the wooden bucket and climbed down to the foot of the cliff where she cut the witch's head off and carried it away in the bucket.

When the king saw the witch's head, he gave Mutzmag one thousand dollars in twenty-dollar gold pieces. Then, he asked Mutzmag if she would like to make another thousand dollars.

"If you can't kill that giant," he said, "I'll be just as happy if you can get me my horse back."

"He keeps it in a barn up the hollow from his house," said the king. "He's got ropes all over that horse and bells all over the ropes. If you move the horse, he can hear the bells."

"Well, I can give it a try," said Mutzmag.

That night, under the cover of darkness, Mutzmag returned to the cabin. When she heard the black dog barking, she continued on up the hollow to the barn where she found Ten-Mile Stepper in his stall. Mutzmag began to cut the bells from the ropes tied to the horse with her case-knife. Suddenly, the giant was behind her. He had become suspicious when the black dog had barked. He grabbed Mutzmag.

"What are you going to do with me?" said Mutzmag.

"I'm gonna kill you," said the giant.

"How?" said Mutzmag.

"I ain't thought about it yet," said the giant.

"Well, please don't put me in a sack," said Mutzmag. "Don't beat the sack with a club because I'll howl like a dog, and my bones will break like dishes cracking, and my blood will run like honey!"

"I should have thought of that myself," said the giant. "That's just what I'll do!" Then he laughed.

The giant dragged Mutzmag to the house and pushed her into a burlap sack. Then he hung the sack from a hook in the ceiling. The giant went off to find a club. Outside the cabin, he unchained the dog to guard against Mutzmag's escape.

When the giant was gone, Mutzmag cut a hole in the sack with her case-knife. She cut the rope that held the sack. Then she put the giant's honey-jar and his dishes in the sack. Using her ball of string and some sticks, she placed the sack in front of the door with the opening propped open like a funnel. Finally, she shouted at the dog, "Come and get me!" and opened the door. The angry dog ran straight into the sack. Mutzmag closed the sack, tied it with the rope and hung it from the ceiling hook. Then she escaped through the back door.

When the giant returned, he had a great club which he had cut in the woods.

"I got you in the sack," he said, "and I'm gonna kill you and you are gonna howl like a dog." The giant hit the sack and the dog howled.

"Now your bones are gonna crackle and pop like a pile of dishes breaking!" The giant hit the sack and the dishes broke.

"Now your blood is gonna flow like honey!" he said as he continued to beat the sack. When the honey ran from the sack and dripped on the floor, the giant noticed that the "blood" was really honey. He realized that he had been tricked.

The giant heard Mutzmag ride down the hollow on Ten-Mile Stepper. He grabbed his rope from the sack and rushed after Mutzmag.

Coming to the river, Mutzmag rode upstream until she found a shallow crossing. She crossed over and rode back down the opposite bank until she was at the river's deepest point. Then, she waited for the giant.

Seeing Mutzmag on the opposite bank, the giant was puzzled. "How did you get across?" he said.

Mutzmag skipped a stone across the river. "I skipped myself across," she said. "Find a big rock, tie a rope around it, put it around your neck and then throw the rock in the river."

"I should have thought of that myself," said the giant, and he did as Mutzmag suggested. When he threw the rock in the river, he was jerked after it and drowned. Mutzmag rode Ten-Mile Stepper back to the king and queen's house and collected her second one thousand dollars.

The king and queen were so glad to be rid of the witch and the giant, and have Ten-Mile Stepper back home, they gave Mutzmag land adjoining their own so she could build herself a house. She lives there now, in a pretty white farmhouse with a chimney on either end and blue trim around the windows. Most evenings, she sits on her porch and talks to her neighbors, the king and queen.

If you need help getting rid of giants and witches, just look her up. With the help of a case-knife, a ball of string and a little imagination, she can probably help you out.

9

Rapunzel, Rapunzel

Once upon a time there was a garden, and in it grew a plant called rapunzel. The garden belonged to a witch of great power and no one dared enter it for fear of their life.

A man and his wife lived near the garden. The woman was expecting a child, and as the time of the birth grew near, the woman began to crave the plant that grew in the witch's garden. She begged her husband to get it for her, saying that she might die for want of it.

One dark night, the husband went to the garden and stole the plant for his wife. Before he could escape across the wall, the witch discovered him.

"How dare you come into my garden and steal my rapunzel," she said. "You must be punished."

The man pleaded with the witch, explaining that his wife felt she must have the plant or die.

"Take it, then!" said the witch. "Take all you want, but there is a condition. You will give me the child that your wife shall bear."

The man wept in despair.

"It will be well treated," said the witch. "I will care for it like a mother."

In his terror the man consented to everything and when the child was born the witch took her. For twelve years she kept the little girl with her. Then she locked her in a tower deep in the forest and kept her there for nearly two years. She called the child "Rapunzel" after the plant in her garden.

The tower had neither a door nor stairs but only a little window in the very top. Each day, the witch would come to the foot of the tower and call out, "*Rapunzel, Rapunzel, let down your hair!*" Each day, Rapunzel let down her hair and the witch would climb up to her window. And so they lived, the girl and the witch.

But one day, a young prince, riding through the forest heard the witch call Rapunzel. He watched as the girl dropped her long hair from the tower window, and he saw the witch climb up. Waiting until the witch had left, the young prince called out, "*Rapunzel, Rapunzel, let down your hair!*" Then he climbed up to Rapunzel's window.

At first, Rapunzel was frightened to discover—not her old mother—but a young, handsome man. The prince spoke softly to her, assuring her that she had nothing to fear. Rapunzel found she loved his company and when he asked if he could come again, she agreed. And so it was, that the witch came by day and the prince came by night. Rapunzel and the prince planned to be wed. Each time he came, he brought a skein of silk so that she might weave a ladder for her escape from the tower.

One day when the old witch climbed through the window, Rapunzel said, "Why is it, Mother, that it takes you so long to get up here when my young man is here in a moment?"

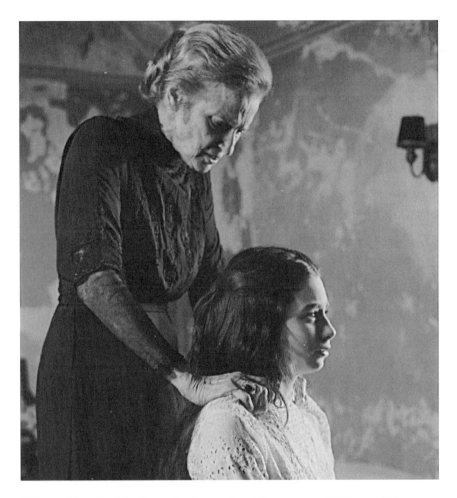

The old witch's face darkened with anger. "What did you say, child?"

Too late, Rapunzel realized she had made a mistake. Frightened, she admitted that she was visited by a young prince.

"Wicked, wicked child!" said the witch. "You have deceived me. I meant to keep you hidden from the whole world. Now you must be punished." Seizing Rapunzel's hair, she wound it around her left hand and cut it with a pair of scissors and the braids fell on the floor. Then she sent Rapunzel far away to a desert place.

That night when the prince called out, "*Rapunzel, Rapunzel, let down your hair,*" the long braids fell as always from the little window. But when he climbed through the tower window, instead of Rapunzel, he found the witch waiting for him.

"So you thought to find your lady love, did you?" said the witch. "Well, she has flown away and you will never see her again. The cat has taken her away, and now she will scratch out your eyes, too!"

In despair, the prince leaped through the window and fell into a great thicket of brambles at the foot of the tower. The fall did not kill him but the brambles blinded him. He wandered through the forest, living on roots and berries and wailing for the lost Rapunzel.

Years later, he came to the desert place where Rapunzel was living. He heard a voice that sounded familiar and suddenly he felt Rapunzel's arms about him. As she wept for the blind prince, two of her tears touched his eyes and he could see again. The prince led Rapunzel back to his kingdom and there they lived happily ever afterward.

10

Soldier Jack

When the great war came, Jack joined and went to fight overseas. He fought here and he fought there, and when the war ended, Jack was discharged and sent home. Back in those days, the government didn't pay soldiers a whole lot. All Jack had when he got off the train was a couple of sandwiches to keep him going until he found a job and a place to stay. But lots of folks were worse off than Jack. When he got off the train, a beggar asked him for money.

"Hey mister, could you spare some change for a cup of coffee and maybe something to eat?" said the beggar.

Well, Jack didn't have any money, but he had two sandwiches. He gave the beggar one of them. After traveling all day, Jack became hungry. He sat down to eat his remaining sandwich. At that moment, a little old man appeared beside him and stared hungrily at the sandwich. Jack gave the little man half of his sandwich, and he immediately devoured it. Realizing that the man was starving, Jack said, "I gave a fellow down the road a whole sandwich, but I only gave you half, so here, you can have it all."

The little man took the food, and said, "Now, I have something for you. Sit down." After Jack sat, the man produced a blue jar and a burlap sack.

"Now if you ever want to catch something," he said, "just hold this sack in one hand and slap it with the other. Then say, *Whickety-whack, into my sack*, and it will get right in the sack for you."

The little old man gave Jack the sack. He held up the jar. "If someone is sick, this jar will tell you if that person is going to live or die," he said. "All you have to do is fill the jar with water and hold it up. You look through it and if you see Death standing at the foot of the bed, then you know that person is going to get well. But if you see Death at the head of the bed then, by cracky, you know that person is going to die."

Jack looked at the sack and the jar, not believing anything that the man had said. When he looked up again, the little old man was gone.

As Jack continued his journey, he became very hungry. Finally he sat down and, looking at the sack and the jar in his hand, he decided to throw them away. At that moment, he heard the gobble of wild turkeys coming from the hill above him. Going into the woods, Jack saw three turkeys. Although he did not believe what the old man and told him, Jack struggled to remember the magic phrase. He held the sack open and said, "*Whickety-whack, into my sack!*"

To Jack's amazement, the three turkeys flew into the open sack! Slinging the sack over his shoulder, Jack continued his journey. After a while, he came to a small town. Finding the local cafe, Jack succeeded in exchanging the turkeys for a meal, a place to stay and fifty cents besides.

The following day, Jack continued his journey. In the afternoon, he found himself before an old farm. It looked as

though it had once been a nice place, but now the land was untended and the house looked bleak and lonely. Jack found a sign posted on the fence that said, "Free House. Inquire at Drugstore. Mr. Bliven." On the bottom of the sign, someone had added, "Not Responsible for Mishaps on Premises." Looking at the property, Jack decided that the place suited him, so he returned to town and found Mr. Bliven.

"I saw your sign down the road," Jack said. Are you really going to give away that house?"

"You get the whole farm," said Mr. Bliven, "and a thousand dollars to boot!"

"What do I have to do?" said Jack.

"Well, you have to spend one night in the house," said Mr. Bliven. "The place is haunted."

Well, Jack laughed at that. "You mean ghosts and all?" he said.

Mr. Bliven nodded. "We are trying to find someone who can break the haunt."

"Well, I would like to try," said Jack.

Jack and Mr. Bliven returned to the deserted farm. The druggist explained that there was something that was worse than ghosts in the house. He said that the townspeople were worried about it spreading beyond the house.

"I've been overseas with the war and all," said Jack. "I saw some pretty rough stuff, so I don't scare easy."

"Them other fellers didn't either," said Mr. Bliven. "They spent the whole night, too."

"Why didn't you give them the farm and the money?" asked Jack.

"Because, when I came out here the next morning," said Mr. Bliven, "they were dead as a doornail!" He pointed to three graves near the house.

"Like I said, I don't scare easy," said Jack. "I'll see you in the morning."

When Mr. Bliven was gone, Jack entered the farm house. The druggist had given him some food and supplies, so he set about making himself at home. After a supper of beans and crackers, Jack lay down in a corner and went to sleep.

Several hours later, Jack awoke to find three green devils with wings staring at him. At first, he was frightened, but then one of the demons gave him a pack of cards and indicated that they wished to play. Seeing that he was not in any immediate danger, Jack agreed to play poker with the demons. Jack kept losing and he suspected that the demons were cheating. Finally Jack said,

"I've only got this dime left." Then he thought about the three grave stones behind the house, and he said, "Did you play cards with those other three fellas?"

The demons nodded.

Jack's fear returned. "What happened to them when they ran out of money?" he said. The demons drew swords and showed them to him. Jack ran. Upstairs and downstairs, he fled with the demons in hot pursuit. Suddenly, seeing his sack in the corner, he grabbed it, and turning to the demons he said, "*Whickety-whack, into my sack!*" The demons jumped into the sack and Jack tied it shut.

The next morning, Mr. Bliven returned to the house. Since he was certain that Jack was dead, he had brought a coffin and two gravediggers. When they entered the house with the coffin, they found Jack drinking coffee while the demons screamed and hissed in the sack. Jack asked Mr. Bliven and the gravediggers to help him. They took the devils down to the blacksmith and paid him to sledge them until they were just smoke and powder.

Jack got his farm and a thousand dollars. The townspeople were delighted that Jack had removed the haunt from the house, and he became a local hero. Now he had everything that he wanted except a wife.

One day Jack was listening to the radio and he heard that the daughter of the President of the United States was seriously ill. He had seen her picture in a magazine and he had thought that she was the most beautiful woman he had ever seen. So, Jack picked up his sack and his jar and caught the bus for Washington.

When Jack arrived, the President was desperate. All of the world's great doctors had examined his daughter and had been unable to help her. When Jack arrived, he was taken to see the President.

"This man doesn't look like a doctor," said the President. "Where did he come from?"

"Mr. President, he is the only one left," said the bodyguard.

The President stared suspiciously at the sack in Jack's hand.

"Well, you better know what you are doing," said the President.

When Jack entered the daughter's room, he removed the jar from the sack, filled the jar with water and looked through it. He saw Death standing at the head of the bed. The President, who could not see Death, became alarmed by Jack's strange behavior. Before Jack could open the sack, the President said, "Get this man out of here! He is a fool!"

As he was being dragged from the room, Jack managed to escape. Running back into the room, he locked the door, grabbed his sack and said, "*Whickety-whack, into my sack!*"

The President sent for his armed guards but before they could break into the room, Jack unlocked the door and walked out with the daughter. Naturally, the President was astonished and thankful.

The President thanked Jack in a national ceremony and gave him a Medal of Honor. Jack married the President's daughter and became a national hero. When he returned home, he took the sack with Death in it and hung it in a tree. After a while everybody forgot about it. The seasons changed, the years went by and folks got older and older. But they didn't seem to notice because without Death in the world, it's hard to mark time. Jack took care of the house and did some light farming. Time passed. Then it passed some more.

One day Jack met an old woman on the road near his farm. Being sociable, as Jack always was, he asked the old woman how she was getting along.

"Oh Lord, son, it's awful," she said. "I'm 206 years old. How old are you?"

Jack thought a minute and realized he couldn't remember how old he was. He asked the old woman, "Do you want to die?"

"Oh yes, son. Of course I do! It ain't natural to live as long as I have."

"Well, why can't you die?" said Jack who had forgotten all about the sack.

"Why ain't you heard?" said the old woman. "Some blamed fool tied Death in a sack. Ain't nobody died around here for over 150 years. Ain't natural," she grumbled.

"No," said Jack, "that isn't natural." Then he remembered what he had done with Death so long ago. It took him a while, but he found the tree, and there on the top-most limb, the sack was still hanging.

Jack found a young boy and paid him to climb the tree, cut the sack loose and bring it down. When the boy handed Jack the sack, he sat down and untied the rope that held the mouth of the sack shut. Then, he let Death out.

Of course, Jack was the first one that Death took.

3/93

mlib